JUST ME AND MY LITTLE SISTER

BY MERCER MAYER

A GOLDEN BOOK • NEW YORK
Western Publishing Company, Inc., Racine, Wisconsin 53404

My little sister wanted to go to the park. Mom was too busy, so I said, "I'll take her."

So we went to the park,
just me and my little sister.

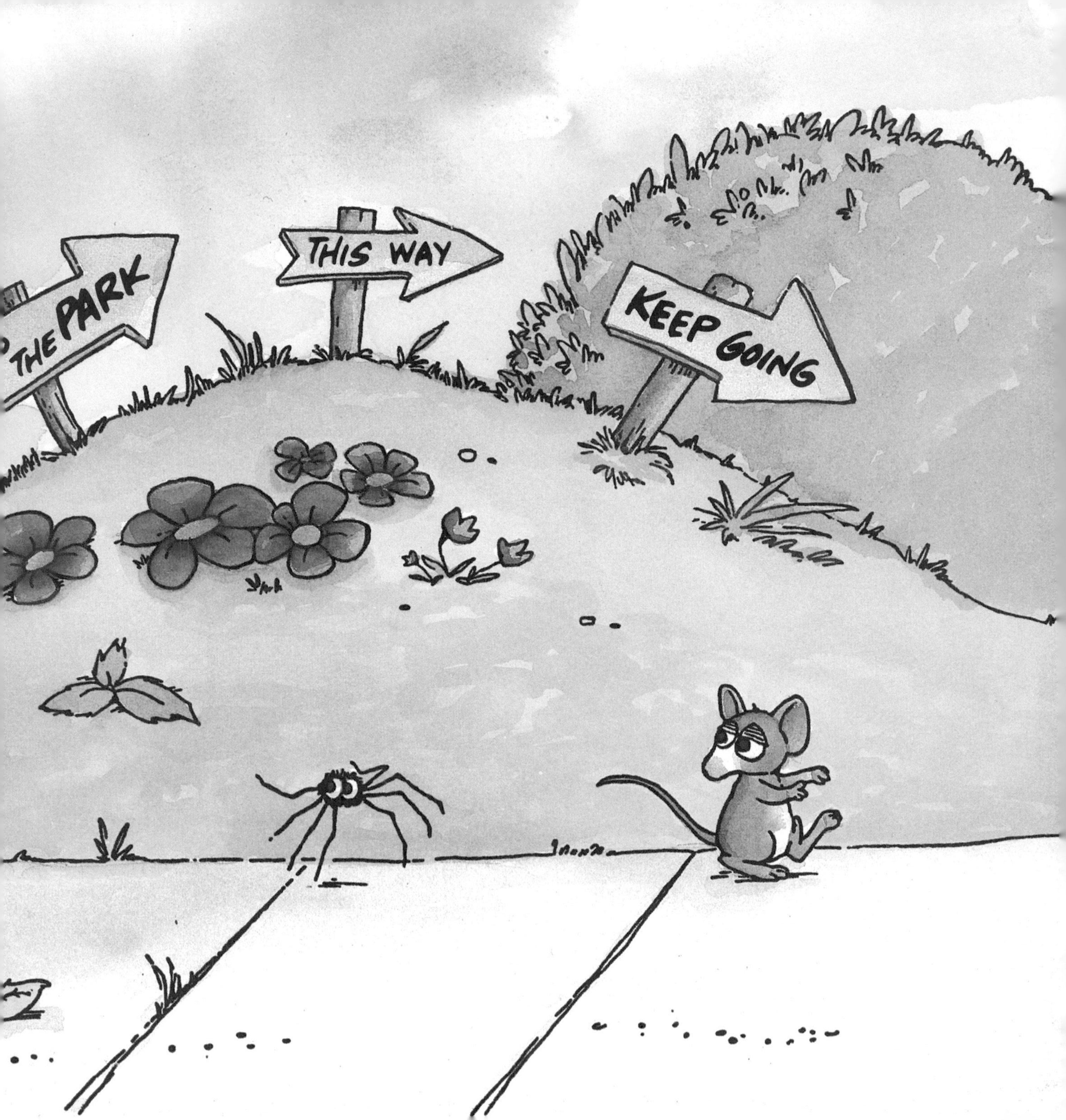
THE PARK
THIS WAY
KEEP GOING

My little sister wanted to play basketball,
but the hoop was too high.

She wanted to play jumprope,

so I showed her how.

Then she wanted to play hide and seek,
but she got lost.

My little sister climbed to the top
of the jungle gym.

I had to help her get down.

She wanted to go on the big slide,
so I caught her at the bottom.

I gave her a ride on the merry-go-round,

but it went too fast.

So I let her go on the swing
until she was tired.

Then she was thirsty,
so I helped her drink from the fountain.

My little sister went to the sandbox.
She wanted to play mudpies . . .

. . . but it was time to go home.

My little sister had such a good time at the park that Mom says I can take her again tomorrow.